BLACK STAR,
BRIGHT DAWN

Scott O'Dell

Houghton Mifflin Company
Boston

Library of Congress Cataloging-in-Publication Data

O'Dell, Scott
  Black Star, Bright Dawn.

  Summary: Bright Dawn must face the challenge
of the Iditarod dog sled race alone when her
father is injured.
  1. Iditarod Trail Sled Dog Race, Alaska —
Juvenile fiction. 2. Eskimos — Juvenile
fiction. 3. Indians of North America — Juvenile
fiction. [1. Iditarod Trail Sled Dog Race,
Alaska — Fiction. 2. Sled dog racing — Fiction.
3. Eskimos — Fiction. 4. Indians of North
America — Fiction] I. Title.
PZ7.0237Bm 1988   [Fic]   87-35351
ISBN 0-395-47778-6

Printed in the United States of America

QUM 20 19 18 17

This story is dedicated to the brave legions of mushers, women and men, who have run the Iditarod, the grueling dog sled race across two vast mountain ranges and the Yukon River, against fifty-mile-an-hour blizzards, in temperatures of sixty degrees below, for more than a thousand miles, from Anchorage on the Gulf of Alaska to Nome on the icebound Bering Sea. And to the magnificent dogs who pulled their sleds.

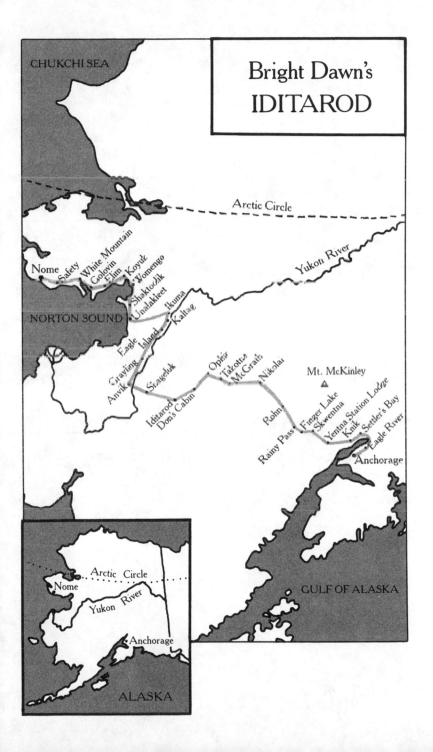

Bright Dawn's
IDITAROD

CHUKCHI SEA

Arctic Circle

Nome
Safety
White Mountain
Golovin
Elim
Koyuk
Womengo
Shaktoolik
Unalakleet
Ikuma
Kaltag
Yukon River

NORTON SOUND

Eagle
Island
Grayling
Anvik
Shageluk
Iditarod
Don's Cabin
Ophir
Takotna
McGrath
Nikolai

Mt. McKinley

Rohn
Rainy Pass
Finger Lake
Skwentna
Yentna Station Lodge
Knik
Settler's Bay
Eagle River
Anchorage

GULF OF ALASKA

Arctic Circle
Nome
Yukon River
Anchorage

ALASKA

BLACK STAR,
BRIGHT DAWN

1

On the tenth day of November the sun did not rise. This was the day the sea froze up and there were no more waves. All the birds, except the ravens, flew south and we would not see them again until spring. It was very cold. The air was so still you could hear people talking far away at the end of the village.

My father did not go out on the ice that day. It was thick enough to hold a man's weight, but he waited two days, then three, hoping that leads, streaks of open water, would appear. This is the best time to hunt in the kayak, the little canoe made of deerskin.

After the third day and the streaks of open water had not appeared, a blizzard blew from the north and lasted for almost a week. It brought floating ice down from the Bering Sea, and the polar ice pounded against the ice along the shore.

Bartok, my father, decided not to wait for the leads to open. He told me to get the dog sled and harness the dogs. He would hunt without a kayak.

"We'll hunt bearded seals on the ice," he said.

Bearded seals are heavy. They can weigh six hundred pounds. I harnessed our seven dogs to the sled and chose Black Star to lead the team. Bartok did not like him. When Black Star was a year old, my father decided that he would never in this world make a good leader.

"He's stubborn," my father said. "You tell him something and he does something else."

"He's smart," I said, remembering the winter when we were coming home and, just on the other side of Salmon Creek, Black Star pulled up and wouldn't move. My father took the whip to him and still he wouldn't move. Then my father walked out on the frozen creek and fell through the ice up to his neck. I remembered this time but said nothing about it. "Black Star knows a lot," I said.

"Of the wrong things," Bartok said. "He's got too much wolf in him. His father came from Baffin Bay and had a lot of wolf blood. They bred him to a Siberian husky. So he's mostly wolf."

I liked Black Star. I had liked him since he was a month old. There were seven in the litter and he was the most playful of them all. He bounced

2

around and took nothing from his brothers and sisters, giving two bites for every one he got.

He was of the purest white, with a black star on his forehead and black slashes under big eyes. But of everything, it was his eyes themselves that captured me.

They were ice blue, the color of the ice that floats down from the Bering Sea on the days when the sun is at its tallest. At first I thought how cold and suspicious and wild they were, looking at me from a world I had never seen and would never know.

After a while, I felt that behind this look was a shadow of friendship. That changed and I saw nothing but friendliness. Then that changed, too. Sometimes, when moon shadows were on the trail and we were hauling things down from the forest, the wild look would come back again.

Before I harnessed him to the sled, Black Star went down the gang line, his bushy tail curled over his back. His ears pricked forward. I had seen a motion picture one time at school about a parade in Washington. There were soldiers standing in a line and a captain walking along, stopping to look at each one of them. Black Star reminded me of the captain, only when he stopped, he reached out and gave the dogs a sharp bite on the ear.

"I tried hard to break him of that," my father said.

"He wants the team to know that he's the leader."

"Yes, but they know he's the leader without having their ears bitten off. Maybe you can do something with him."

"I'll try," but I liked Black Star the way he was.

"You could harness him up first. That way he won't have a chance to go along biting ears."

"You tried that once, remember? And it didn't work at all."

"I don't remember."

My father could forget something he didn't wish to remember. Now he didn't want to remember that he had used a whip on Black Star. He was a strong-willed man, but the dog was strong-willed, too. He was silent as Black Star went down the line biting ears, all the while watching the caribou whip.

"There isn't a cloud in the sky. What a fine day to hunt," I said.

Last winter my father had killed only three bearded seals and there was a whole month when we didn't have much to eat. Hunting would be better this year, my father said. He was good at telling how far south the seals would go on their summer travels — a thousand or two thousand miles — and when they would return to the cold waters of Womengo.

The full moon was rising. There were scratchy clouds far down in the west, but it would be a fine

4

day. Bartok got out his hunting things, put them on the sled, and got in beside them.

"We hunted the south shore last year. Bad luck," he said. "Maybe we should hunt north this year. What do you think?"

"North," I said, eager to go in any direction.

My mother took her time to answer. She was wearing a parka she had made in the summer of fox fur and wolverine. She looked very pretty.

"South was bad hunting last year," she said, handing Bartok some smoked salmon strips to eat while he was out on the ice. "So it should not be bad this year again."

"No, I am sure," Bartok said. "Last night I had a strange dream. I was gathering clams along the shore. Out of the sea came a bearded seal. He was very thin and could barely move on his flippers.

"'I have come a long way,' he said. 'I am starving. Will you give me some of your clams?'

"I was about to say that I needed them for my family. Then I saw that each of his ears was a gleaming pearl. At once, I knew that it was the King of the Bearded Seals.

"'You can have all of the clams — there are more than two dozen — if you make me a promise,' I said.

"'I am starving. I'll promise anything, Bartok Machina.' (He knew me, he called my true name.)

5

"'Then promise that you'll have some of your subjects, many of them, visit our shore this winter.'

"'A hundred. Two hundred.'

"With that, he scooped up the clams, swallowed them in one gulp, and waddled fast into the sea."

Every year this sort of talk went on between him and my mother, Mary K. When he went out on the ice they would always talk this way and always about a dream he'd had.

There was a reason for such talk. Hunting is dangerous. Danger lurks everywhere. Killer whales are thirty feet long, and if a man is hunting in a kayak they can snatch him up, kayak and all. If it's angry, a Kodiak bear can kill a hunter with a single swipe of its paw. Polar bears are the worst of all. They feed on seals, and because hunters always smell of seals, the bears think they are seals and track them down. A hunter does not go out on the ice without fear. But he is not a man unless he does go.

Women never hunt. My father was even criticized for letting me drive his sled to the ice, to help him bring back the seals he took. Women's place was at home.

I had been doing it now for two winters. It started when my brother was killed on the ice, the day he speared a bearded seal with the harpoon rope looped around his neck and was dragged into the depths and drowned. In my father's eyes,

somehow I became his son who had died on the ice.

The hunters in the village and their wives did not like me to go out with my father. It made no difference to him. For a long time now I had driven the sled to the ice and helped him load the heavy seals on the sled, and driven back home. Often we drove down the village street in broad daylight so everyone could see us.

2

Smoke from breakfast fires hung above the village. Men were starting off toward the south. My father and I went north. We went along the shore, hunting for a good place to go out on the sea.

During the freeze-up, polar ice was driven down through the Bering Strait by north winds and struck the shore. The collision flung up great mounds and spires and ridges, mixed with sand and rock. These *eewoonucks* formed an icy wilderness between the shore and the frozen sea.

It took us nearly an hour to find a place to hunt. We staked out the dogs and climbed a jagged ridge. My father saw the head of a bearded seal, just the top of it, sticking up through the ice. The seal sank out of sight when it saw us.

My father climbed down from the ridge and gathered up his things — his knife and his harpoon with the long rope fastened to it. He followed the ridge until he came close to the stretch of flat

ice and the breathing hole where the seal had shown its head.

Between my father and the hole was a narrow bridge of ice. He got down on his hands and knees and crawled slowly from one side to the other. Seals have good ears. They can hear footsteps many yards away through the ice.

I watched him crawl to the lip of the breathing hole and not move for a while. He coiled the long rope harpoon. Then he crouched beside the hole a step away, his legs braced, his body bent forward, and the harpoon in his hand.

My father was the best hunter in our village. It was because he was very patient. He could crouch for hours this way, bent over, waiting for a seal to show its head. Often he waited for half a day, sometimes for a whole day, and when I brought him food he wouldn't eat it for fear he would not be ready with the harpoon.

There was so much waiting that I always brought schoolbooks to read. In this way I was able to keep up with my studies. My teacher, Helen Tarrana, was good about letting me make up the time I lost. But today it was so cold, the pages wanted to stick together. I did manage to read about the golden seal, which does not inhabit our waters. Her fur jacket is made of hairs so fine that three hundred thousand are packed into one square inch so that she's always warm and waterproof.

Imagine! Who counted all these hairs? I wondered.

Books can be exciting, useful too. My mother named me out of a book she was reading the morning of the night I was born. It was about seals, the beautiful creatures who live in two worlds. She came to a place in the book where, in the deepest of a sunless winter, for some strange reason, a day dawned bright, bright as a day in spring. That is how I got the name. Bright Dawn.

I closed my book, climbed down from the ridge, and fed the dogs, who were restless. Then I climbed back up and kept an eye on my father. He had not moved. He looked like an ice statue crouching there among the *eewoonucks*.

The moon was full. By late morning its light began to fade. A south wind came up and shifted around to the north. It was much colder now. I climbed down and built a fire and warmed myself. Then I climbed back up the ridge. Bartok still hadn't changed his position beside the breathing hole.

The seal had another hole somewhere, I decided. Seals can't stay down for much more than five minutes before they have to come up for air.

The wind died and it started to snow, large flakes at first, then small ones that had ice on the edges. We were miles from home. Part of the distance was through the *eewoonucks*. I called to my father to give up the hunt. He did not answer. By now he looked like a snowman.

I called again. Slowly he raised a hand to quiet me. The snow was coming down harder, but it was very still, except that from far off I heard the rumbling of shelf ice.

I climbed down from the ridge, taking my time. It was very slippery. The dogs were lumps in the snow. I scraped them off, searched around for driftwood, and tried to build up the fire. I had no watch, but I was good at telling the time of day. It must be an hour after noon, I decided.

The fire would not burn and from a cloudy sky the moon cast only weak shadows. But I found my way along the path Bartok had taken. It was hard to see. I got down on my hands and knees and crawled to the edge of the shelf and groped along to the bridge that connected the shelf to the polar ice.

It was not there. Instead, I saw a jagged point sticking up like a spear. Beyond, I caught a glimpse of blue water, the sea.

I cupped my hands and shouted. The wind flung the shout back in my face. Was my father on a floe that was drifting away from the shore? Had he come back to the bridge, found it gone, and taken another way to reach the shore? Wherever he was, I would never find him.

I went back to the camp, harnessed the dogs,

and started off against the raging wind. The *ee-woonucks* all looked alike. I did not try to find the way back to shore. Knowing that I would never find it, I walked along beside Black Star and let him guide us.

When we were near home, Mary K. heard us and was at the door. She was calm. Mothers and wives were always calm when bad news came. They were trained to hear bad news. Not a winter went by that at least one of our men was not lost on the ice.

Mary K. hurried into her parka. My feet were wet, beginning to freeze, so I changed my socks and boots and we ran up the road, spreading the news through the village. All the women and the old men came out and followed us to the outpost store.

Anvo Noorvik, the man who owned the store, said, "Nothing can be done until the hunters come in from the ice."

We knew that.

He looked at his watch. "Six o'clock," he announced. "Some will be back in an hour. Everyone will be back in two hours. In two hours we will start the search. Now we will return to what we were doing."

When we came in, Noorvik was opening a box with a pry bar. The bar was still in his hand. He gave the box a jab as we filed out.

Everyone wanted to take us into their homes, but my mother refused. We walked into the blizzard, heading along against it, through the village to our home. But we felt better, having been with our friends.

3

The first thing I did when we got home was to tie a leather rope across the room under the ceiling.

If a rope goes limp, my father had told me, it's a sign that the hunter is in danger. If it goes limp more than a little, if it hangs down, then the hunter is dead. Then the clothes that hang behind the stove to warm him when he comes in are taken down and put away forever.

An hour went by. The rope did not move. The blizzard piled snow against the windows. It shut out the light, so I lit candles. My mother busied herself over the stove. She did not believe in the rope. She had gone to a school in Nome where they did not like what they called Eskimo superstitions.

When we heard dogs barking in the village, I ran outside and started toward the store. The blizzard was at my back and I went fast.

Most of the men were home from the ice, more

than twenty of them. They had heard the news from Anvo Noorvik, but they wanted to know it from me. I told them what had happened, leaving out nothing that I thought would help. They hugged the hot stove and were silent. I wondered if they would ever thaw out and talk.

At last, squat, lank-haired Utak Tuktu, who was a good hunter, said, "Now we go to look for Bartok."

"To find him," Louis Katchatag said.

"And bring Bartok home," someone said. "He is safe. He is friends with the ice for a long time."

I asked Tuktu if I could go with him. He didn't bother to answer.

Hunting on the ice was not something for girls or women. This I knew well, but I asked him again as the men filed out. Again, he didn't bother to answer.

They took four dog sleds and nine kayaks. I followed them down the road and saw them disappear in the driving snow.

When I got home, my mother was watching the deerskin rope, even though she said she didn't believe in it. "It hasn't moved a bit," she said. "It still hangs tight."

We cooked supper and ate some of it. The blizzard had stopped. I cleaned the snow off the window so we could keep track of the weather. The moon shone in a cloudless sky.

Around midnight we heard dogs barking in the village. I went up the road to see what it was. The last of the hunters were returning from the ice with the seals they had killed.

We divided the time; my mother slept for an hour, then I slept. Toward morning, while I was watching the deerskin rope, I saw it move, or thought I did. I got my mother and she sat down and watched, too.

"I see nothing," she said, a little angry with me for believing. "You are tired. Your eyes are tired."

"They are not tired," I said, begging her pardon.

We watched together for a while. Then I got up and made breakfast, a big one, pan bread and all. Ten long hours and more had passed since the men had gone out. My father could be coming home now.

An hour past noon a sled came up from the south. I ran out, thinking it might be a sled bringing my father home, but it went on to the village. When I got there, they were carrying Louis Katchatag into the store. He had fallen into open water and was covered with thick ice, even his face.

After he was thawed out, Katchatag told us that my father had been sighted. He was on a large ice floe moving slowly north past the village. The hunters thought they could reach him in a few hours if the wind didn't move the ice floe away from the shore.

16

I went home and told my mother what I had heard. It was good news, but she said nothing, getting up to look out the window, coming back to keep an eye on the deerskin rope.

Neighbors brought food, special food like caribou steak, that they knew Bartok liked.

The wind came up and slapped hard against the house, against one wall, then another. We couldn't tell what direction it was blowing from. It blew cold air down the chimney and filled the room with so much smoke that we couldn't see the stretched rope.

I got out a pair of my father's best mukluks, the ones made from sealskin bleached in winter weather, soft and almost white. I had made the tops. They had patterns of different-color fur and bands of wolf fish skin. They looked fancy.

Boots are as good as ropes for telling how things are.

I hung them up by the window, where I could see them clearly in the moonlight. As long as the boots move, even a little, if they walk, the hunter is alive. If they stop walking, the hunter will never, ever wear them again in this life.

Hunters drove by on sleds and went to the store to thaw out and eat. I cooked food for them. All the women cooked food. The men were hungry. Jack Eagle ate three thick caribou steaks and a loaf of bread before he went back to the ice.

17

The news was good. Whenever the snow let up they had caught glimpses of my father. He was still on the big floe and it was moving along the shore, not out to sea. That day, if they could steer a kayak through the fields of floating ice — they had lost five kayaks already — they would reach the floe and bring my father home.

4

Late that night, we heard sleds on the road far to the south. They came closer, passed our house, and we ran after them.

The hunters carried my father into the store. He was stretched out on one of the kayaks. They put him down by the fire and covered him with a robe. He said nothing.

"He's doing pretty good," Anvo Noorvik said. "But he's got a bad hand. It's frozen. Turning black. He needs a doctor."

There was a heavy silence while Anvo Noorvik went into his office and started up his radio. Crackling sounds and sputtering voices were all we heard for what seemed like an hour. It could have been half an hour.

I stood beside my father. He was under a mound of fur robes and I couldn't see any part of him. I spoke to him and he said a few words that I didn't understand. They sounded as though they came up out of a deep hole.

Anvo Noorvik said, "I got Doc Evans. He's over in Grassy Creek working on broken legs. He'll be here in six hours or less, depending on the weather."

John Evans was the only doctor between Womengo and Nome. He traveled around, making regular calls at fishing villages along the Sound. Dr. Evans had saved many lives.

Driving his team of six malamutes, he reached the store at gray dawn and operated on my father. He had to take off all the fingers on Bartok's right hand, all except his thumb.

"Your husband is a strong man," Dr. Evans said to my mother as he left to go up the Sound to Ovakoff. "The worst is over."

We took my father home, but the worst was not over. His hand healed, but there was something strange about him.

About two weeks later, I was sitting by the window, working on the sealskin boots I sold to people in Nome who sold them to visitors in the summer. Our house was on the shore and the window faced westward to the sea.

My father glanced out at the jumbled spires of the *eewoonucks*. With a groan, he yanked the curtain shut, plunging the room into darkness.

I got up and lit a lamp. As I walked back to the

table where I was working, the light shone in my father's face. His eyes were two deep hollows. His mouth was twisted to one side. His bronze skin was pale underneath. For a moment I thought I was looking at a ghost.

That day he ate little of the food we cooked for him. That night I heard him talking in his sleep. I could not make out what he was saying, though it was loud, so fearsome that the sled dogs on the porch stopped their singing. They did not raise their voices again that night.

My father was the chief man of our village. He was called *an-yai-yu-kok,* the one that everyone listens to. Everyone did listen to him. But two days later, on the morning the elders met to talk about problems, he did not appear. They thought he had forgotten to come, so they sent a messenger to our home to remind him.

When the messenger knocked on our door, my father did not answer. He sent me, saying, "Tell them that Bartok has a fever in his head."

He was silent. He sat all day with his back to the window and stared and said nothing. Whenever the big ice floes drifted down from the north and crashed onshore, making thunderous sounds, he would tremble and turn pale.

Early in February the elders decided that the village should have a new *an-yai-yu-kok.* My father hadn't been to the meetings for a long while. They chose a new man whom everyone listened to, but said nothing to Bartok about it.

Then Dr. Evans came on one of his visits to the village. He was surprised at what we told him. How my father had quit going to the council meetings, that he never left the house, that he kept the window closed and sat with his back to it, how he trembled whenever sounds drifted in from the frozen sea.

Dr. Evans motioned for Mother and me to go outside. It was a warm day and he stood in the yard with the hood of his parka thrown back. He was tall and broad-shouldered and towered over us.

In a doctor's voice, he said, "I have seen a dozen cases like this before. Hunters who were caught on floating ice and drifted for days, for a week, not knowing at what hour they would freeze to death, afraid to sleep for fear they will not wake up. Others who fell into the sea by accident, who would have died in minutes from the cold had they not been rescued. Not one of these men ever hunted again. It's a phobia."

The sled dogs were barking, eager to be back on the trail. Suddenly they were silent. Bartok had come out to the shed and was listening to us.

My mother had never heard the word "phobia" before. I could tell that it startled her. I had heard it used in school about mad animals, but it startled me, too.

"Fear," Dr. Evans said, "is powerful."

"My husband has hunted since he was a boy," my mother said. "He is not a fearful man."

"Deep down, all hunters are fearful," the doctor said. "But your husband is fearful now, every minute of his life."

"What will happen? What can we do?" my mother said.

"Hard as it may be, it's best that you leave the village and go where this man cannot hear or look at the sea or even smell it. I know of a place. Ikuma. It is on the big river, where fishing and hunting are good. Ikuma has a good school, a better school than here. I am going there next week. I will find you a place to live."

My father came out of the shed huddled up in his parka and turned away from the sea, blinking in the wan light, smiling a wan smile.

Three days later we moved to Ikuma, forty miles from the seacoast. We hadn't much to move — the pot-bellied stove, cooking pans, dishes, knives and forks, a barrel of smoked salmon, a barrel of seal meat, and the six caribou skins we slept on.

We piled everything on the big sled and Bartok drove. He stood straight on the runners. He looked almost the way he did before those days on the floating ice. The dogs were eager to go.

Mary K. and I got on the sled and covered ourselves with one of the caribou skins. My father

cracked his whip. It curled around the dogs' ears.
When we came to the hill that looks down on our
village, my mother glanced back.

"Bartok was born in Womengo," she said quietly.
"And his mother and father were born in Womengo. Their mothers and fathers were born in
Womengo. It is sad that we will not see our village
ever again."

"You will like the new place," I said, though I felt
sad, too, and I had no idea what the new place
would be like.

My father cracked his long whip again. He
shouted at the dogs and did not look back at the
village or the frozen sea.

5

Ikuma was not a village like Womengo. It had more than a thousand people, a post office, two cafés, and three stores besides a trading post.

At first, we lived on the far side of the river, at the edge of the tundra, a great treeless place. Our makeshift house was made of birches bent over and tied at the tops and covered with caribou skins. After a year, after my father got well and found work with the Empire Canning Company, we moved to a house in town and I had my own room, the first one I'd ever had.

The school was much bigger than the school in Womengo. There were three teachers. Helen Grammas taught English and history, such as the Constitution and the Revolutionary War. Ellen Dusek taught arithmetic. John Seward taught geography and other things.

There was also a church where the Reverend Cartwright told us about God and the Devil, about heaven and hellfire. I got mixed up listening to him, because I had always believed in the God Sila.

Sila is a mystery. He lives far apart from us, way off in nothingness. No one has ever seen him. No one has ever heard him speak. But he watches to see that we do not harm the world we live in — the air and water, our friends the animals, the land and the sky. If we do harm them he will become angry and all of us will vanish from the earth like mist in the morning.

John Seward encouraged us to play games. He led the school band and taught me to play the trumpet. Dog sledding was a very popular sport. The school had two sleds, three dogs to the sled, and he taught us how to race. He could do everything.

The Yukon is a wonderful river for sleds. It winds back and forth like a mammoth snake. And in places it is more than a mile wide. When the ice is covered with a light snow and the dogs can get a footing, the sleds fly.

I was the only student in school who owned a dog team, but in the town there were dozens, and most of them raced on Saturdays.

Usually the races were thirty miles long. The prizes were merchandise from the stores and meals at the two cafés. I never won, but I did finish every race and came in second twice. I won a dinner at the Blue Goose Café and once a glass cooking dish.

My father didn't like his job at the Empire Canning Company. They canned salmon in the spring, but this was deep winter. The big tin building was deserted. All Bartok had to do was to be a watchman for three hours, six days a week, and look out for prowlers. It was a lonely job, walking around empty tables and silent machinery. When he got home, he never had much to say.

"Why don't you go out like Bright Dawn does and race the dogs?" Mother asked him one night.

My father frowned. "Dogs are meant for work, not for racing."

"They are trained to do both," I said.

He gave the supper table a blow with his big fists. They set the dishes to rattling. "For work, not for play," he said.

But we kept at him. Every night at supper we brought up dog sled racing. It took us most of the winter to get him on a sled. We were not surprised that he came in third in his first race and won a pair of beaded mukluks. In the next race he came in first and won a new parka.

After that he was on the river every Saturday and I didn't have a chance to race until spring. He was very short and had a bow in both his legs, but he was strong. In the bad places he jumped off the sled and pushed and kept pushing for an hour, even with his bad hand. He grasped the caribou whip with only his thumb and sent it singing along the backs of our seven sled dogs. He won six races, then the big one, the three hundred mile race, and $500.

Ikuma was a check station on the Iditarod, the famous dog sled race that starts in Anchorage on the Gulf of Alaska, crosses rivers, vast stretches of frozen tundra, two great mountain ranges, and ends in Nome, on the Bering Sea, after 1,179 perilous miles.

At Ikuma, drivers check in and out. Their times are kept in a book and sent by radio from one checkpoint to the next. In that way it is known which drivers are first and which are last and which in between.

The Iditarod was a big event in Ikuma, the biggest of the whole year. People talked about it months before it happened. I played a horn in the school band. Two weeks before the racers came through the town, we practiced on Yukon Street, marched up and down, and got ready to greet them.

The mushers came on the nineteenth of March. It had taken them more than thirteen days to travel from Anchorage to Ikuma. They still had to travel one hundred and seven miles to reach Nome.

The night before they came and even the night before that, I couldn't sleep. I had heard about the Iditarod for years. In Womengo people talked about it, but I never thought that I would stand in a crowd somewhere and watch the race. I had never dreamed in my wildest dreams that someday I would march in a band playing my silver horn, wearing a spring parka trimmed with wolverine fur, and welcome racers of the famous Iditarod.

It snowed hard all day on the nineteenth of March, but everyone in Ikuma was waiting on Yukon Street when our school band gathered in front of the Gem Café and welcomed the first drivers with "God Bless America" and "America the Beautiful."

Seventy-one mushers had started from Anchorage, we heard, but only thirty-five arrived in Ikuma. The rest had dropped out.

They checked in, one after the other, for three days. On the third night, the last driver that appeared was a girl. She staggered when she got off her sled. She looked so cold and bedraggled that I invited her to come home with me. She smiled weakly.

Her name was Deborah Reed. She was about nineteen, a year or two older than I, and came from Penobscot in Maine.

My mother cooked a hearty meal for her, but she didn't eat it. All she wanted to do was sleep.

"For how long?" I asked her.

"Forever," she said.

"There's hot water. Do you want a bath?"

"Sleep," she said.

"Are you going to give up?"

She thought for a moment, then shook her head.

"When do you want to leave?"

"Wake me in five hours, please."

She fell asleep in the chair. She had frostbite on her cheeks.

I went outside and fed her dogs. I kept track of the time and got her up in five hours. She ate two bowls of soup, and I made her some moose sandwiches.

"I've run in some races," I told her. "But they were nothing like the Iditarod, of course. Tell me about the Iditarod."

"You bounce along on a rough trail," she said. "Sometimes on no trail at all. A wild wind blows in your face and the temperature is forty below. With the wind, it could be one hundred below. You freeze and think you are going to die and wish you would. You sleep four hours a day. You wake up and make a fire and feed a dozen dogs. You examine their feet and legs and boots. You harness them to a towline. It snows. The snow turns into a blizzard.

"Comes another day. It's the same but different. You climb a steep hill, too steep for the dogs, so you get off the sled and push. The dogs want to lie

down. You urge them on. Over the hill the trail plunges down, back and forth. You stand on the brake. You put out the snow anchor, but the sled races on while you grit your teeth. Then there's another day. The same but not the same."

Her face was pale under the skin that the cold had blackened.

The sun came up and she got on her sled. The dogs lunged against their harness. I watched her disappear in the falling snow. With all my heart, despite what she had told me, I wished I was on the sled racing for Nome.

Then something strange happened. That night while we were eating supper, Bill Weiss, president of the Empire Canning Company, and Frank Gibson, owner of the Gem Café, appeared.

"Every year," Mr. Weiss said to us, "we enter a driver in the Iditarod."

"We have entered six drivers, but none of them has won," Mr. Gibson said. "In fact, none of them has ever finished the race. It's not very good for Ikuma. Gives Ikuma a bad name."

Mr. Weiss said to my father, "We've heard about the races you've been winning around here."

"Quite a record you've established," Mr. Gibson said.

"We've been wondering if we could enter you in next year's Iditarod," Mr. Weiss said suddenly.

My father was startled.

Mr. Gibson said, "The first prize is fifty thousand dollars. There are other prizes, too. One hundred and fifty thousand in prizes."

My father was silent. Money did not mean anything to him. He thought the white man was crazy, talking money all the time. If my father could gather warm parkas for his family, boots that kept the water out, dry wood for the stove, enough seal and fish to last the winter, then he was a happy man and made us happy.

Mr. Weiss seemed to know this. He was half Eskimo and half Tlingit Indian. It was the Tlingit part that had made him rich.

"It's not the money so much," he said. "It's the test. In the Iditarod a man finds out who he is and what he is. It's a test of bravery."

My father rubbed his bad hand against his chin, a sudden glint in his eyes.

Then Frank Gibson said that they would pay for everything — supplies, food for the driver, food for the dogs, food drops at the checkpoints. "Everything. A dog team, if necessary."

"It takes a year to train for the Iditarod," Mr. Weiss said. "You'll be on the payroll of the Empire Canning Company, the same as always, but you'll spend ten hours a day on the trail, getting your team in shape."

My father was dumbfounded. He stared at the two men.

Mr. Weiss said, "You should start training tomorrow."

My father sat and stared.

6

Early the next morning a sled drove up in front of our house. A man with a gray beard got off the runners. He came to the door and spoke to my father.

"My name is Peter Avakoff," he said. "I've been hired to help you get ready for the Iditarod. I've raced in two of them. Came in fifth and tenth. Raced in the last one, too, but my heart acted up and I had to drop out."

My father was still recovering from the shock Mr. Weiss and Mr. Gibson had dealt him the night before.

"Are you ready?" Peter Avakoff said.

My father didn't answer. He was out the door, dragging me along. Together we harnessed up our dogs.

"I need weight," he said. "What do you weigh, Bright Dawn?"

"One hundred and twenty-nine pounds," I said.

"Jump in," my father said.

He sent the caribou whip snaking along the dogs' backs and we were off for the river, Peter Avakoff and his team running beside us.

We ran twenty slow miles down the river, then stopped for Peter Avakoff to rest and talk about the Iditarod, how it was different from all the other dog sled races. When we got back, he came into the house and talked again.

My father, who had never learned to write, asked me to put down everything, word for word, as Peter Avakoff talked. How to pass another team on the trail and keep your dogs from fighting the other team. How often to feed the dogs. How much — not all they could eat — and what food was best. Water was very important. How often they should drink and how much, surely not all they could.

My father had seven dogs on his team.

"You need twice that number," Peter Avakoff said. "You'll lose dogs along the way, virus and accidents. You have to finish the race with seven at least."

It took only a day for Mr. Weiss to find more good dogs, trained dogs that had raced before.

After that, the two men went out every day and four times a week at night, because a lot of the Iditarod was run at night. I went with them on Saturdays.

I took down what Peter Avakoff said. By summer I had a small book of notes. Every week my father asked me to read them over to him from the beginning.

When the ice on the big river broke up, he and Peter Avakoff took their teams into the hills north of the village, where deep snow still lay on the ground. They trained all summer, though most of the snow had melted by July, going out days and nights and traveling at least fifty miles each time.

After most of the snow had melted, there were stretches of mudholes and quivering ground that shook and bounced the sled. It wasn't much fun, but Peter Avakoff told my father that he would encounter lots of mudholes in the Iditarod and it was a good idea to get used to them.

In November, John Seward put the two dog sleds from the school together, borrowed another team from the Trading Post, and entered me and my friend Julia Englet in the three-hundred-mile Ikuma–Nome Express Race. We were out for four days and had fun but came in twenty-first and twenty-second.

It was the next month, after a heavy snow had fallen, that my father and I had the terrible accident.

Early one Sunday we were out on the trail. My

father tried to pass Peter Avakoff's team. Our sled was bouncing, and I was holding on tight with both hands. We were halfway past the other team. Our dogs were barking at his dogs. Bartok snaked out the long caribou whip.

Now we were past them. We were about to swing back onto the trail and Peter Avakoff shouted, "Good."

The dogs were kicking snow in our faces. Suddenly our sled slipped to one side of the trail, then to the other, but it didn't straighten out. It rose in the air, came down, rose again, tipped, skated along on one runner, and crashed against a tree.

My father was on his feet before I got to him. We were both dazed and covered with snow. Peter Avakoff untangled our dogs. We got the sled right side up and headed back home. Bartok made a joke about the accident, but he looked so pale that I knew he was injured.

Ikuma did not have a doctor. We had a good veterinarian, though. Dr. Goshaw looked at Bartok and took X-rays and said that his left shoulder was cracked in two places. He wound it up with yards of tape, made a sling, and gave Bartok some medicine, which he didn't take.

Mr. Weiss and Mr. Gibson came while we were eating supper. They had heard about the accident and talked to the veterinarian.

My father jumped up from the table and made

37

a show of being in fine shape. "Three weeks and I'll be back," he shouted.

Mr. Weiss gave him a sharp look. "That's not what we hear. The vet says you'll be laid up for six weeks, maybe longer."

Mr. Gibson said, "That's too bad."

"Terrible," Mr. Weiss said.

Both men were sympathetic, but I felt that already they had made up their minds that Bartok would not get well in time for the race.

"Three weeks and I'll be back," my father said, still shouting, swinging an arm to show them how strong he was.

"Say you are back in three weeks," Mr. Gibson said. "That will be the middle of January. The race starts early in March. Your team needs to run fifty miles a day to get in shape. That's more than a thousand miles gone, lost, down the drain."

"Bright Dawn will train the dogs for me," my father said. "She's a good trainer."

"But what if your shoulder doesn't heal in three weeks?" Mr. Weiss asked. "What if it takes six weeks? Two months, the vet says. What happens then?"

My father didn't answer.

"Well, I will tell you what happens," Mr. Weiss went on. "We've spent more than twenty thousand dollars on fees, food for you, food for the dogs,

38

food drops here in Ikuma and other checkpoints. On the best sled money can buy. On seven trained malamutes that alone cost us forty-two hundred dollars. We've spent all that money, and there we would be on the day the race starts with no one to race. Do you get the point?"

My father sat down at the table. Then he got up and strode across the room and looked out the window at the falling snow. Then he came back and sat down again. He did not answer Mr. Weiss.

In the lamplight his cheeks had a rosy glow, but his hands, clenched in a knot, were white. He glanced at me, started to say something, and stopped.

For a long while there were no sounds in the room except the crackling of wood in the big stove.

Then Mr. Weiss said, "These are the facts, Bartok. What do you think we should do? Wait and see what happens? Gamble that you'll get well in a month or six weeks? What?"

It seemed terribly hard for my father to answer. Words came out of his mouth slowly. "My daughter will run the race," he said.

Mr. Weiss and Mr. Gibson were startled. They looked at each other, then at me.

Mr. Weiss said, "But your daughter's too young. She's still in school."

"A schoolgirl," Mr. Gibson said.

I could say nothing. I was overwhelmed by the thought of racing in the Iditarod. Then I got all of my wits together in a hurry.

"I am not a schoolgirl," I said. "I graduated from school the tenth of this month. I have a diploma. There it is on the wall."

I pointed. The men turned and glanced at the diploma.

"And I am not a girl. I'm eighteen years old. I'm a woman."

"Women have won the Iditarod. Two of them," my father said. "They weren't much older than my daughter."

"I know, I know," Mr. Weiss said.

Mr. Gibson said nothing.

They put on their parkas. As they left, Mr. Weiss said, "You will hear from us. Soon."

It was not soon. A day went by. Almost two days went by. I gave up hope on the second day, but my father told me that he had had a vision.

"They will come tonight," he said. "They have decided. You will run in the big race."

"Will I win? Will I win?"

He thought. "The vision is not clear about the winning part."

Mr. Weiss and Mr. Gibson came while we were eating supper. They took off their parkas. They stood by the stove and warmed their hands and said nothing. I poured two mugs of coffee for